ON THE

SPEEDWAY

BY JAKE MADDOX

ILLUSTRATED BY SEAN TIFFANY

Jake Maddox books are published by Stone Arch Books
A Capstone Imprint
151 Good Counsel Drive, P.O. Box 669
Mankato, Minnesota 56002
www.capstonepub.com

First published in 2010 by Stone Arch Books as:
Pit Crew Crunch
Race Car Rival
Speed Camp
Stock Car Sabotage

Library of Congress Cataloging-in-Publication Data is available on
the Library of Congress website.

ISBN: 978-1-4342-3030-0
Summary: Four stories about auto racing.

Printed in China.
092010
005926

TABLE OF CONTENTS

PIT CREW CRUNCH

TEXT BY
L. TRUMBAUER

PETER GRANGER

**Car 3
Team Jimmy Turner
Position: Pit Crew**

TABLE OF CONTENTS

Chapter 1

THE CONTEST

As soon as he got home from school, Peter ran to the mailbox. He flipped open the white metal lid and carefully slid out the mail.

Nothing. Still no letter from the NASCAR officials.

While flipping through a magazine the month before, Peter had seen an interesting ad. The ad announced a new NASCAR contest.

The winner would be able to work on a pit crew for one of the major race car drivers of NASCAR! All Peter had to do was write a short essay, fill out some information, and send in his entry.

Peter couldn't believe his luck. He loved NASCAR more than anything. Winning the contest would be a dream come true.

He knew a lot of kids would enter. But he figured he had a good chance anyway, since he loved NASCAR so much.

He'd given it his best try. He had filled out the form right away and sent it in that very same day.

I think NASCAR is the best sport around! Peter had written. *You have to know how to handle a car. You have to understand engines, tires, and tracks.*

NASCAR is more than just knowing the rules. It's about knowing the mechanics of cars and racing, too.

With my love for cars and racing, I think I'd be an excellent member of any pit crew.

It wasn't hard to explain why he loved NASCAR. The hard part was waiting to find out if he'd won. What was taking the selection committee so long to make a decision?

Peter headed back to the house. He kicked the gravel on the driveway.

He'd been so certain that the notice would come today. After all, it had been almost a month since he sent in the form.

As he walked up the front steps of his house, he heard the phone ring. Peter ran inside and answered it.

"Is this Mr. Peter Granger?" asked a man's voice.

Peter clutched the receiver. "Um, yes. Yes, it is!" he said.

"Mr. Granger, this is Lee Harlow at NASCAR headquarters," the man said. "We are pleased to announce that your contest entry was one of only a few chosen out of several thousands."

Peter gulped. "It was?" he asked.

"Yes!" Mr. Harlow said. "You may be able to work in a pit crew during a NASCAR race!"

Chapter 2

TESTS

Peter couldn't believe it. He'd actually won the contest! "This is awesome!" he told Mr. Harlow.

"I'm sorry it took us so long to call you and tell you that you'd won," Mr. Harlow said. "I hope it was worth the wait!"

"It definitely was!" Peter said.

"Good. I'll be sending you some forms to sign. I'll also send you some information about NASCAR," Mr. Harlow said.

"Information?" Peter repeated. "But I already know pretty much everything about NASCAR."

"Yes, but there are rules about working in the pit crew," Mr. Harlow explained. "We can't just let anyone behind the scenes of a NASCAR race. You'll have to pass a few tests first."

Peter hadn't thought of that. "So it will be a while before I'll actually work the crew," he said.

"Not too long," Mr. Harlow said. "Take a look at the information I'm sending, and see what you think."

Peter didn't need to look at the information to decide. He knew he'd do whatever it took to be able to work on the pit crew. He'd dreamed of being part of a NASCAR race for his whole life. He wasn't going to blow this chance.

After Peter hung up the phone, he called his best friend, Kurt. Kurt was just as excited about the pit crew spot as Peter. Peter told him everything Mr. Harlow had said.

"What do you think the tests will be about?" Kurt asked.

"I have no idea, but I'm sure I can pass them, whatever they are," Peter said. "Will you help me?"

"Of course," said Kurt. "But I don't think you need to worry. You know more about NASCAR than anybody, except maybe your dad. You'll definitely pass the tests."

* * *

Another week went by. Peter checked the mail every day. Finally, there was a thick envelope from Mr. Harlow inside the mailbox.

The envelope contained some forms for Peter and his dad to sign. Mr. Harlow had also sent a lot of information about NASCAR and about working on a pit crew. Peter read all of the information really carefully.

The biggest problem Peter knew he had was that he'd never worked on a real car before. The pit crew preferred members who were experienced. Working on the crew was not easy.

Peter knew it would take practice and hard work. He wasn't afraid of that. He was just worried that he didn't have the right skills to join the crew.

He'd won the contest, but that didn't guarantee him a spot in the pit crew. He hadn't realized when he entered the NASCAR contest that he'd have to pass so many tests.

"I wonder how many more kids have been chosen," Peter said to Kurt.

"Why don't you call Mr. Harlow," Kurt suggested. "I bet he could tell you."

"That's a great idea!" Peter said. He found Mr. Harlow's phone number and called him up.

Mr. Harlow answered the phone right away. He told Peter that four other people had been chosen as possible candidates for joining the pit crew. They all needed to go to the racetrack in two weeks to take the tests.

"I really want the spot, Mr. Harlow," Peter said.

"I like your eagerness, Peter. Just be prepared when you come to the racetrack," Mr. Harlow told him. "We'll see then if you've got what it takes."

Chapter 3

HELP FROM DAD

On Sunday, Peter and his dad planned to watch a NASCAR race together. Peter loved watching the races and hanging out with his dad. It would be the perfect time to tell his dad about the contest.

Just before the race began, Peter brought all of the information from Mr. Harlow into the TV room. His father was sitting down with a bowl of chips and a soda, getting ready to watch the race.

"Hey, Dad, look at this," said Peter. He handed his father a copy of the essay he'd written about NASCAR.

"Is this for school?" Dad asked.

"No," said Peter. "It's for NASCAR."

"NASCAR?" his dad repeated. He frowned and read the essay.

Peter explained how he had entered the contest. "Four other people won, besides me," he said. "Now I have to pass a test to be on the pit crew. So what do you think, Dad?"

"Well, I'm not sure," his father said.

Peter took a deep breath. He remembered what Mr. Harlow had said on the phone. Peter needed to show that he could be a great pit crew member.

"I was wondering if maybe you could help me," Peter said. "I need to learn how to change tires and jack up the car. And maybe you could show me how to quickly screw in the lug nuts and stuff."

"So if you pass the tests, then you get to join the NASCAR pit crew?" his father asked.

"That's what Mr. Harlow told me," Peter said. "He said to meet him next Saturday at the track here in town."

Peter's dad was silent for a moment. The only sound in the room came from the NASCAR announcer on the TV.

Finally, Dad said, "It sounds like a great opportunity."

Peter was once again afraid to breathe. "And?" he said.

"And I think you should definitely go for it," his father said.

"All right!" Peter said.

"This is going to be a lot of hard work," his father said. "None of it is going to be easy."

"I'm ready for it!" Peter said. "I feel like I've been ready my entire life!"

"Okay then," his father said. "Let's take notes during this race. Then we'll go out to the garage. We'll see what you can learn on my car."

Then Peter and his father watched the NASCAR race. Together, they paid close attention to the pit crew. In fact, they watched the pit crew more than they watched the cars!

They looked at the second hand on the wall clock in the TV room.

They timed how long the pit crew took to change tires, tighten nuts, and jack up the car to look for damage. It only took the crew a few seconds to do all of that work.

Peter felt nervous watching the pit crew fly through their tasks. How could he ever work that fast?

That week, with his father's help, Peter learned how to change a flat tire. His father timed him as Peter jacked up the car and loosened the lug nuts.

They went to the gas station. There, they timed how quickly Peter could inflate tires.

By the end of the week, Peter felt like he was ready. He was ready to face his competition.

* * *

On Saturday, Dad and Kurt went to the track with him. When they arrived, Peter looked around. Some other guys were there, talking about the contest. Peter guessed that they were the other NASCAR fans who had won the essay contest.

He hadn't expected all of the other guys to be so much older. They were also a lot bigger.

Peter felt like a little kid compared to the other guys. His confidence drained away.

Chapter 4

NOT SO BAD

"Peter, did this contest have an age requirement?" Peter's dad asked.

"It said thirteen and up," Peter said. "I thought a lot of other thirteen-year-old guys like me would enter too."

"Do you recognize any of these guys?" Dad asked.

Peter shrugged. "No. They must be in high school," he said.

"In what grade? Fifteenth?" Dad joked.

"I'm sure they haven't practiced as much as you have," Kurt said. "You've been working really hard. You don't have anything to worry about."

"I hope you're right," Peter said nervously.

Just then, a man in a denim jacket and jeans walked over. "You must be Peter Granger," the man said.

"And you must be Mr. Harlow," Peter said. He stuck out his hand, and Mr. Harlow shook it. "It's nice to meet you," Peter added.

"The pleasure is mine," Mr. Harlow said, smiling. "I'm always glad to meet NASCAR fans. Now, let's get started! Come on over here."

Peter's dad and Kurt went to watch from the stands. Peter and the other contest winners introduced themselves. Peter had been right. The other guys were all in high school. He was the youngest guy there.

"The first thing you'll have you do is take a written test," Mr. Harlow said.

Some of the older guys groaned. Mr. Harlow chuckled. "Don't worry, guys, this isn't like school," he said. "This will help us figure out how much you know about NASCAR and about racing."

Peter and the other four essay contest winners spread out in the bleachers to take the test. It wasn't the most comfortable place to take a test, but it sure beat sitting in a classroom.

Peter hadn't been expecting a written test. Still, the test was pretty easy. There wasn't a single question he couldn't answer.

Peter knew that NASCAR had started from old bootleggers in the south. He knew that NASCAR stood for the National Association for Stock Car Auto Racing.

He also knew that the start of the NASCAR season actually began with the Daytona 500 in Daytona Beach, Florida. He would bet that a lot of people didn't know that. Most people would probably assume that the racing season was like the football season. They might figure that the Daytona 500 was kind of like the Super Bowl. But Peter knew that it was held at the beginning of the racing season, not at the end.

Twenty minutes later, Peter handed in his test. He was the first one done. He knew so much about NASCAR that he was sure that he could have answered even more questions.

While he waited for the other guys to finish their tests, he sat back, nervously tapping his feet. He wanted to show those guys that he could work in a pit crew. He wanted to show them how quick he could be and how strong he was.

He might have been smaller and younger than the other guys, but he was ready for the challenge. He knew he could do it.

Soon, all the tests had been collected. It was time for the next trial.

Mr. Harlow assigned each contestant a number. Peter was given the number 3. For the next challenge, they had to pay attention to five race cars zooming around the track.

When the contestant's numbered car pulled into the stop, the contestant was supposed to hop over the wall and assist. The contestant would take his instructions from the pit crew already there.

Only seven people were allowed to work "over the wall." That was the spot where the race car slowed down and stopped for servicing.

The pit crew was responsible for refueling the car and for putting air in the tires and changing them if needed. The pit crew also had to recognize any damage and fix it, if possible.

Sometimes the pit crew also helped the driver by making sure he had water to drink.

All these tasks took time, but the pit crew had to work very quickly. They only had fifteen seconds. After that, the car had to start moving again.

Peter waited behind the wall. He watched as the cars zipped along. He looked at the number 3 car.

Finally, the number 3 car was slowing down! Now was his chance!

Peter flung himself over the wall.

Chapter 5

SHOW YOUR STUFF

Peter couldn't believe he was standing next to an actual race car. Oh, sure, it probably wasn't like the official cars that had to pass qualifying races to enter a big NASCAR race. But he was as close as he had ever gotten to one!

Peter was surprised when one of the pit crew members threw him a helmet and a pair of gloves.

"Safety first!" the guy said.

Peter jammed everything on as quickly as possible. *Am I being timed for getting dressed, too?* he wondered nervously.

Then he flew into action. Before he knew it, he was pumping air into tires. He was washing windshields. He was helping to secure lug nuts.

Peter could feel the blood rushing through his veins. His hands didn't shake at all as they handled the equipment.

The equipment wasn't exactly like what he'd practiced on at home. How could it be? He'd practiced on a normal car, and this was a race car. But the equipment still felt right in his hands. Peter's hands seemed to move all on their own. It was like he'd been working in a pit crew forever.

He loved every minute of it — from the smell of the oil and grease to the feel of the warmth of the race car. The six other crew members did their jobs quickly. Everything worked together perfectly, down to the last lug nut.

Soon, the car was once again ready to roll. Peter was tired, but thrilled. Working on the race car had been one of the best moments of his life.

As he stood there, catching his breath, Peter watched the number 3 car ease down the track. The car slowed and stopped.

Busy in the pit crew, Peter hadn't noticed the car's driver. Peter had been too focused on the car. Now he watched as a familiar form emerged.

It was Jimmy Turner.

Jimmy Turner was a master race car driver. He had won several Daytona 500 races. He even starred in a few TV commercials. Jimmy Turner was a king of the racetrack. And he was one of Peter's biggest idols.

Jimmy Turner waved at Peter. "Come on over!" he called.

Peter's hands began to sweat. He placed his gloves and helmet on the wall. Then he walked over to Jimmy.

"Good going, kid!" Jimmy said. "Was that really your first pit crew?"

Peter gulped. "Um, yes. I mean, I practiced with my dad in our garage," he added.

Jimmy laughed. "In your garage?" he asked.

"That's right," Peter said. "But it doesn't really prepare you for the real thing."

"Not exactly," Jimmy said. "Even so, I think you did a fine job."

"Really?" Peter asked. He smiled.

"I'll talk to Mr. Harlow, but I'd like to have you on my crew at least once this year," Jimmy told him. "What do you say?"

"What do I say?" Peter said. What could he say? "I'd love it!"

Chapter 6

HARDER THAN BEFORE

Peter brought Jimmy over to meet his dad and Kurt. Peter's father reached out to shake hands with the race car driver. "It's a pleasure to meet you," Dad said. "Peter and I have spent many hours watching you race."

"Thanks," Jimmy said, smiling. "It was a pleasure to have your son on my crew today."

"He's a hard worker," Dad said.

"Mr. Turner asked me to work on his pit crew," Peter told his dad.

Jimmy nodded. "Your son did a great job today," he said, "but we still have a ways to go."

"You mean another test?" asked Peter.

"Well, we don't let just anyone work in the pit crew," Jimmy explained. "Besides passing timed tests, each person has to get along with the rest of the crew. And they have to be very hard workers."

Jimmy paused. Then he went on, "The job isn't easy. Lots of people work hard to get here."

"I know Peter would work hard, like everyone else," Dad said.

Jimmy nodded. "He's already shown that he has the ability," he said. "Now we have to see how well he'll be able to work with the team."

Jimmy arranged for Peter to work with the pit crew for the next few Saturdays. Saturday races were usually qualifying races for the drivers. The big events were held on Sundays.

Peter looked forward to every weekend. He loved the rush of the race cars zooming by. He loved the way the crew worked together so the car ran smoothly.

Peter wasn't allowed to work over the wall during the races. But he still helped the pit crew. Instead of jumping over the wall, he'd stand on top of it. That way, he could pass down supplies that the race car driver and the crew needed.

Peter quickly became part of the team. One of the jobs he always did was wiping down the tires. The tires needed to be cleaned off when they got covered in too much gunk. From his perch on the wall, Peter reached down with a long-handled broom. He brushed the gunk off the tires.

He was also a big help to the driver. He found a bucket and attached it to a broom handle. He filled the bucket with water bottles.

From the wall, Peter reached the bucket toward Jimmy. Then all Jimmy had to do was lean over and grab the bottles.

The heat, the noise, the crowd! Peter loved it. He didn't think there was any better place to spend a Saturday than a busy racetrack.

Then one Saturday, Jimmy walked over to Peter after the race.

"Peter, can you work the pit crew tomorrow?" Jimmy asked.

Peter's mouth dropped. He couldn't believe it. "Seriously?" he asked. "During the real race?"

Jimmy nodded. "I think you're ready," he said. "Now, let's go find you a pit crew suit."

Chapter 7

THE WALL

Peter could barely sleep that night. He was too busy thinking about brushing tires and tightening lug nuts.

He got to the track early on Sunday morning. His dad and Kurt headed into the bleachers to watch the race.

Because of Peter's age and his size, he still wasn't allowed to work over the wall. He'd be working on the wall, like he did during the qualifying races.

He was disappointed. At the same time, he also knew he was as close as he'd possibly get to a real NASCAR race.

As Peter slipped his safety suit on, Jimmy walked up.

"The race is about to start," Jimmy said. "Do you think you're ready for your big debut?"

"Yes, sir. I wish I could work over the wall with the pit crew," Peter said. "But I know I'm safer on the wall."

"No one's ever put someone your age over the wall before," Jimmy explained. "So let's see how you do on the wall first."

"Okay," Peter said. "Good luck out there today!"

Jimmy walked away. Then Peter started setting up.

He got his tools ready for the race. His giant broom was ready to wipe down the tires. The bucket was full of water bottles to pass to the driver.

Soon, the race was about to begin. The crowd was getting louder and rowdier.

Peter climbed onto the pit crew wall. He dangled his feet over the side. Within seconds, the race began.

Peter kicked his heels against the pit crew wall as he watched the race. The cars zoomed around the track.

He kept his eyes on Jimmy's green and white car, the one with number 3 painted on the side in black paint. All of a sudden, the car quickly edged out of the pack of dozens of cars.

Jimmy Turner was making a move!

Peter held his breath. In the audience, people started pointing to Jimmy Turner's race car.

Peter checked his watch. He glanced at the giant wall clock near the pit crew station.

It was almost time for Jimmy Turner to pull over. His tires needed air and rubbing down. Parts had to be checked.

And Jimmy was probably hot — really hot — inside his race car. Peter knew that the temperature inside a race car could be more than 100 degrees. Jimmy would need a drink of cold water as soon as he pulled into the pit.

Peter watched as the green-and-white car slowed down. It neared the pit. It slid to a stop behind the wall.

Peter got ready to stand up. He was prepared.

The first thing he'd do would be to lean over and run his broom across the surface of the car's dirty tires.

Peter started to get to his feet. Then, suddenly, everything went wrong.

Chapter 8

CAR HOODS

In all the weeks Peter had worked with the pit crew, he'd never seen a car leave the track and drive into the wall. The movement was completely unexpected.

One minute, Peter had been standing on the wall. The next moment, the wall shook and he was airborne.

Then his feet slammed into the hood of the race car.

Peter's entire body seemed to jostle and grind. The race car shook like crazy beneath him.

Somehow, Peter still managed to hold onto the broom and the bottle of ice water. He didn't drop anything.

Jimmy flung himself out of the car. "What do you think you're doing?" he shouted up at Peter.

Peter felt like he'd been punched in the gut. He'd hit the car really hard. He couldn't seem to find his breath.

"I fell," Peter said.

"That's pretty obvious," Jimmy said.

The pit crew had gone into emergency mode. Peter's father came jogging up. Kurt was right behind him. They had prime seats in the infield.

Dad and Kurt had seen everything — from Peter climbing the wall to Peter nearly getting crushed by the race car. Dad looked really worried.

Peter was glad he was wearing the safety suit. If it hadn't been for all of the extra padding, he was sure his body would be in a million pieces.

"I hope I didn't smash up the car too much," he said to Mark, the head of the pit crew.

"Let's get you up off that hood and see what damage was done — to you and the car," Mark replied. "With luck, both of you will be okay. That was quite the fall you just took."

Dad reached out his hands. He helped Peter get off the hood.

Peter turned to look at the car. The hood still seemed sturdy. There weren't any dents or bumps or cracks. That was good news.

Peter's back hurt, but the car was fine. But Jimmy still looked upset. His face was red, and he wouldn't look at Peter.

Suddenly, a stretcher appeared at the side of the race car. Peter heard a cheer go up in the grandstands and in the infield. He realized that the audience was cheering for him. They were cheering because Peter was able to move.

Peter let his father and Kurt help him onto the stretcher. Peter was afraid to look at the pit crew.

He was mostly afraid to look at Jimmy. They had all put so much faith in him, despite his age and his size. He knew he had let them down.

Peter leaned back on the stretcher. He watched as the scenery changed overhead. Two ambulance drivers lifted him into the ambulance. Peter listened as the cheering and whistling continued.

Then the ambulance doors slammed shut. Everything was quiet as he rode to the hospital.

Chapter 9

IN THE HOSPITAL

Dad and Kurt met the ambulance at the hospital. After the ambulance drivers rolled Peter into the building, Dad leaned over to give him a hug. Then he stopped. Peter was all banged up, after all. A hug would hurt him more than help.

Even the ride on the stretcher was painful. The stretcher bounced along the winding hospital halls. Peter was sure he'd need X-rays or something. The doctors would have to make sure he hadn't broken anything too seriously.

Peter wiggled his arms and legs. Everything seemed to be working. Sweat began to bead on his forehead. He was starting to feel hot in his suit.

The ambulance drivers wheeled Peter into the emergency room. They brought him to an empty bed. Peter watched as Dad pulled the privacy curtain around his bed. There was a small TV nearby, tuned to the NASCAR race.

"I still don't understand how you managed to get yourself knocked off the wall," Dad said.

Peter wanted to shrug, but it hurt too much. The pain was getting to be unbearable.

"I guess a real race is way different from working the crew at a practice race," Peter said. "I should have practiced falling," he added.

Just then, a bunch of doctors and nurses marched over to Peter's bed. One of the doctors slid a heartbeat monitor over Peter's arm. The other doctors took his temperature and checked his blood pressure. Everything seemed normal.

"I think you just need to rest," one of the nurses said. "And we'll get you out of this suit and into something a little more comfortable."

Peter actually wanted to keep wearing his safety suit. As long as he had it on, he still felt like he was part of the pit crew.

If he changed into the hospital clothes, he'd have to admit that he'd messed up. He'd let Jimmy down.

Just then, the privacy curtain was pushed aside. Peter couldn't believe it when he saw the familiar face. Jimmy Turner walked up to his bed.

"What are you doing here?" Peter asked, shocked. "Shouldn't you be finishing up the race right now?"

"I had to make sure you were okay," Jimmy explained. "I can't let a member of my team go to the hospital without checking on them," he added. "I was worried about you."

Peter looked away from Jimmy. "I guess I'm not part of the team anymore," Peter said sadly. "After what happened today, I mean."

Jimmy frowned. "Who says? It's my decision who works on my team," he told Peter. "Now that we both know what to expect, we'll be more careful. You'll wear more safety gear, for one thing. And we'll keep you behind the wall."

Jimmy continued, "You'll get special equipment so you can still help out, but you'll be safer that way. I don't want to lose one of the hardest-working members of my team."

"Really?" Peter asked happily. "I can keep working on the crew?" He looked over at his dad.

"If we can make sure you're safe, I don't see a problem," Dad said.

Peter smiled. "Yes!" he said. "We can go over all the safety stuff before I work another race."

"Speaking of races, today's is only half over," Jimmy said. "Let's watch the rest. Let's see which bucket of bolts actually wins!"

Peter laughed. The pain he'd felt almost disappeared. He and Jimmy sat back and watched the rest of the race.

RACE CAR RIVAL

TEXT BY CHRIS KREIE

SHAWN LEWIS

SCHEDULE

20

MACBETH

DRIVECAN OIL

Car 20
Team "Mean" Gene Pederson
Position: Junior Member

TABLE OF CONTENTS

Chapter 1

GO-KART GLORY

Shawn Lewis kept his kart just inches behind the go-kart in front of him. He shot down the track straightaway and into the last lap of the race.

"It's time, Freddy," Shawn said to himself. Freddy Stow was racing in the kart ahead of Shawn. "It's time for me to beat you again."

The crowd was going wild. There must have been 500 fans in the stands.

Shawn and the other drivers were competing in the Premiere Tire Cup. It was one of the most important kart races of the season.

The first person to cross the finish line would win $300. They'd also receive four brand new kart tires from Premiere Tire.

Shawn drove hard through the first turn. Then he stayed right behind Freddy's kart through corner number two. The two karts sped down the back straightaway. Just two more corners before they crossed the finish line. The rest of the cars were too far back to catch them.

This is where you always make the same mistake, Freddy, thought Shawn. *You drive too sharp through the third corner and let me pass you.*

The two karts approached the third turn. Shawn took his foot off the accelerator for a split second. He drove his kart to the outside and went wide through the third turn. He positioned himself to drop tight through turn number four.

Everything went just like Shawn had planned. Freddy went sharp into turn three, which forced his kart out wide after the last turn.

Shawn saw his chance and jumped at it. He pushed the pedal all the way to the floor and shot past Freddy on the last turn and into the final straightaway.

Seconds later Shawn crossed the finish line first. "Yes!" shouted Shawn. "I win again!"

After the race, the top three drivers waited in victory lane to receive their trophies. "Good race, Freddy," said Shawn as he put his hand out.

Freddy shook Shawn's hand. "You, too," he said.

"What's it like always coming in second?" Shawn asked, laughing. "We're just like Johnny Pride and 'Mean' Gene Pederson."

Johnny Pride was Shawn's favorite professional stock car racer. He was everyone's favorite. He was young, good looking, and had won the Chase for the Cup three years in a row.

"I'm Johnny. I always finish first," teased Shawn. "And you're Mean Gene. You never seem to win."

Gene Pederson always finished behind Johnny Pride. He didn't have many fans.

In fact, he was the most hated driver in stock car racing. In a race last season, his car had rammed Johnny's into the wall. Johnny had ended up in the hospital, and his fans had never forgiven Mean Gene.

"I'm just joking, Freddy," said Shawn. "You need to smile once in a while. You always look mad, just like Mean Gene."

The boys received their trophies and walked off the track. "Guess where I'm going tomorrow?" said Shawn.

"Where?" asked Freddy.

"To Talladega! To a real NASCAR race!" said Shawn. "My uncle's company is a corporate sponsor. I get to be Johnny Pride's junior team member all week."

Shawn ran toward the track exit with the first-place trophy in his hand.

Chapter 2

AT THE TRACK

"Uncle Roy!" shouted Shawn as he stepped off the bus in front of Talladega Superspeedway.

"Hi, Shawn," said Roy. "Let me get a look at you. You've got to be six inches taller than the last time I saw you."

"Yeah, right, Uncle Roy," said Shawn. "You just saw me a few months ago."

"Doesn't matter," said Roy. "All I know is that you're growing like a weed."

He lifted up Shawn's baseball cap and messed his hair. Shawn grinned and rolled his eyes.

The two unloaded Shawn's bags from the bottom of the bus and walked across the street. "Check out my ride," said Roy.

"Is this yours?" asked Shawn. "Sweet."

The two of them climbed aboard Roy's golf cart. It was built to look like a mini stock car, and it was covered from front to back in Top Shelf Oil Filter logos.

"How do you like working for Top Shelf?" Shawn asked as the two of them cruised toward the speedway.

"It's the best job I've ever had," said Roy. "Plus, they let my favorite nephew be a junior race team member. Can't beat that, right?"

"That's right!" said Shawn.

The two of them drove through a tunnel under the Talladega track. They headed into the middle of the speedway.

"This is awesome, Uncle Roy," said Shawn. "I can't believe I'm here."

"You deserve it, Shawn," said Roy. "Your dad tells me you're becoming quite a racer. You just might end up racing at Talladega one day."

"I like the sound of that," said Shawn. "Then maybe I'd get to race against Johnny Pride."

Uncle Roy steered the golf cart into a large, open garage. He stopped the cart. "Speaking of Johnny Pride," said Shawn. "When do I get to meet him? I can hardly wait."

"Well, there's something I need to tell you," said Roy. "The good news is, you get to be a junior race team member. The bad news is, I couldn't get you on Johnny's team."

"What?" exclaimed Shawn.

"I'm sorry, Shawn," said Roy.

Shawn looked away. He tried to hide his disappointment. "That's okay, Uncle Roy. I know you tried your best," said Shawn. "So if I'm not with Johnny, then whose team am I on?"

"You're on Gene Pederson's team," said Roy, smiling.

"Gene Pederson? Mean Gene?" said Shawn. "You're kidding, right? Uncle Roy, that guy stinks. He never wins. He's a loser."

"Who's a loser?" said a voice from over Shawn's shoulder. Shawn turned around. Standing directly behind him was a tall man dressed in a racing suit.

It was Mean Gene Pederson.

Chapter 3

HISTORY LESSONS

"Hey there," said Gene, sticking out his hand. "I'm Gene Pederson. You must be Shawn, my junior racer."

Shawn suddenly felt nervous. He didn't know what to say.

"Shake the man's hand," said Roy.

"Oh, sorry!" said Shawn, taking Gene's hand.

"Shawn, I'd like to show you around the track," said Gene. "Let's go for a walk."

"Okay," said Shawn.

"Have fun," said Roy. "I'll meet you back here at five. Think you can stay busy until then?"

"Oh, we'll keep him busy," said Gene. "Let's go, Shawn."

Gene headed out of the garage and into the bright sunlight. Shawn followed him.

"So, I hear you're a Johnny Pride fan," said Gene. He led Shawn past rows of semi trailers.

"You could say that," said Shawn. "Sorry about the 'loser' comment back there. I didn't really mean it."

"Forget about it," said Gene. "I can introduce you to Johnny if you'd like."

"Really?" asked Shawn. "Are you serious?"

"Sure," said Gene.

"Because, you know, he's like the best racer in the world," said Shawn, getting excited.

He rattled on. "He's won the cup three years in a row. If he does it again this year, it will be a new record. That will make him even better than Richard Petty."

"You know your stuff, don't you," said Gene. "I've always been a bigger fan of Richard's dad, Lee Petty. He was a much better racer."

"No way!" said Shawn. "They don't call Richard 'The King' for nothing. And if you're going to go back to the early days of racing, you have to say Buck Baker was better than Lee Petty."

"Baker? Are you kidding?" said Gene. "Baker wasn't even as good as Tim Flock or Herb Thomas."

"Well, you're right about that," said Shawn. "Herb Thomas was the man. He would have won a lot more races if he hadn't gotten injured."

Shawn turned his head as six guys dressed in green race suits walked by.

"You sure know a lot about the old timers," said Gene.

"You do too," said Shawn.

"The way I see it," said Gene, "if you don't know the history of your sport, you can't make history. It's important to know how the sport has grown and changed so you know where it's going in the future."

"Good point," said Shawn.

"Come on," said Gene. "Follow me."

Shawn found himself standing right in the middle of Talladega Superspeedway. The track was fifty yards in front of him, just past a short wall. Beyond that stood the grandstand where all the fans would sit on race day.

Shawn was looking at a sight he had only seen on TV. And it was so much better in person.

Chapter 4

IN THE CAR

"This is awesome!" said Shawn.

"Pretty cool the first time you see it, isn't it?" said Gene. "But watch this."

Suddenly a group of eight men jumped over the wall in front of Shawn. They raced out toward the track. Shawn looked to his right. A speeding stock car was coming toward them. It squealed its breaks and came to a sudden stop.

Shawn immediately realized where he was. He was standing next to pit road, the place where the pit crew made important improvements to the cars during a race.

The men in the pits quickly went to work. Two men used huge metal cans to put fuel in the car, one man raised the car up on a jack, and several men changed all four tires. And it all happened in a matter of seconds.

The car dropped back onto the ground and suddenly sped out of sight and back onto the track.

"That's 14.6 seconds," said a man standing in a tower above the pits. He was holding a stop watch. "That's not good enough, boys. We've got to get it under 13 seconds."

"Don't be so hard on the guys, Bob," shouted Gene. He turned to Shawn and said, "Bob's my crew chief. He keeps my team prepared and organized."

The man with the stop watch looked down. "I didn't see you there, Gene," he said. "But if I'm not hard on the crew, you won't win."

"Fair enough," said Gene.

"Let's do it again!" shouted Bob.

"Pretty cool, huh?" said Gene.

"Cool?" said Shawn. "That was the most awesome thing I've ever seen in my life."

"How would you feel about seeing it from the inside?" said Gene.

"What are you talking about?" asked Shawn.

"Want to see how it feels to come in the pits from inside the car?" asked Gene

"Are you serious?" asked Shawn.

"I don't joke," said Gene. He made a serious face. "I'm Mean Gene, remember?" Shawn laughed.

Gene led Shawn over to Bob. "Can you get the modified ready?" Gene asked. "I want to take Shawn out."

"You got it," said Bob. He shouted to the crew. "Somebody bring out the modified right away!"

"What's the modified?" asked Shawn.

"It's a car that I built for my junior racers," said Gene.

"That's awesome," said Shawn.

"It doesn't go as fast as a regular stock car. It also has extra safety features so I can legally have a passenger in the car with me," Gene explained.

"He's the only driver who has one," said Bob. "You're lucky you were picked to be on Gene's team. None of the other junior racers are going to get out on the track."

"Not even Johnny's?" asked Shawn.

"Not even Johnny's," said Bob, laughing.

"Let's gear up!" said Gene.

Shawn sat in the back seat of Gene's modified stock car. He strapped on a helmet.

"Your helmet has headphones built into it," Bob said. "You'll be able to hear Gene talking to you."

As Gene eased the car onto the track, Shawn heard Gene's voice in his headphones. "We'll take the first lap slow," Gene said. "And then I'll drop the hammer and see how fast this car can go."

Gene guided the car gently around the first two turns. But on the back straightaway, he started to accelerate. "In a real race, there would be forty other cars out here, and we'd be going twice as fast," Gene said.

Shawn could feel Gene push the car even faster. Shawn felt a rush. He tried to imagine 100,000 people in the stands cheering for him.

"Okay," said Gene. "We're pulling into the pit."

Gene ran another lap, sped the car around the last corner, then shot onto pit road. He slammed on his breaks, and the crew jumped at the car from out of nowhere.

This time Shawn looked down at his watch as the men did their jobs. Shawn counted to ten, eleven, twelve. Suddenly the car dropped off the jack, and Gene was punching the accelerator. "I think they were faster that time!" shouted Shawn.

"I think you're right," said Gene.

A huge smile covered Shawn's face as Gene pushed the car hard around the track.

Chapter 5

A PIECE OF TRUTH

"I can't wait to meet Johnny," said Shawn as he and Roy rode the golf cart toward the track. It was Shawn's second day at Talladega Superspeedway.

It was also media day. All the racers were at the speedway to answer questions from reporters. Gene had told Shawn that he would introduce him to Johnny Pride today.

"Johnny Pride," said Roy. "Do you ever think about anything else?"

"He's the best, Uncle Roy," said Shawn. "He's going to win four cups in a row. That's never been done before."

"Yeah, I know," said Roy. "The cups are important. But he's not the only racer out there. You got lucky getting placed with Gene. He's a great guy."

"It was cool how he took me on the track with him yesterday," said Shawn.

"No other drivers do that, you know," said Roy.

"I know," said Shawn. "But I still can't forgive him for putting Johnny in the hospital last season. He could have ended Johnny's career."

"I don't think you know the whole story," said Roy. "That accident was proven to be caused by a mechanical failure."

He continued, "Gene didn't crash into Johnny on purpose. Gene felt so bad about that crash, he hired a new crew chief."

"He did?" asked Shawn. "How come they never said that on TV?"

"Because the reporters on TV like to have a bad guy," said Roy. "They want Johnny Pride to have an enemy on the track. It's good for TV ratings. More people watch the races."

"It doesn't matter to me," said Shawn. "I would watch Johnny no matter who he's racing against."

Roy eased the cart to a stop. "Here we are," he said. "Are you ready to meet your hero?"

"I couldn't be more ready," said Shawn as he flashed a big smile.

Chapter 6

MEETING JOHNNY PRIDE

"Pretty crazy, isn't it?" Gene asked Shawn. The two were surrounded by dozens of racers in the middle of the media tent. "I'll go into the next room soon to take questions, but for now, we just have to wait," Gene explained.

"That's okay," said Shawn. He turned and looked through the crowd of racers in the room.

"Looking for Johnny?" asked Gene.

"Sorry," said Shawn.

"Don't worry about it," said Gene. "He's over there." Gene pointed toward a corner of the tent. "Come on."

Gene and Shawn walked through the crowd and across the floor of the media tent. "Hey Johnny," said Gene. "There's someone here I'd like you to meet. This is Shawn Lewis, my junior racer."

Shawn stepped forward. His heart was racing.

Johnny looked at Shawn. "Nice to meet you, bud," said Johnny.

"It's great to meet you, Johnny," said Shawn. He couldn't believe he was actually talking to Johnny Pride.

"So, you're a fan of Mean Gene, huh?" Johnny asked.

"Uh, yeah," said Shawn. He looked back at Gene.

"Actually, Johnny, you're his favorite racer," said Gene.

"Well, that's not a surprise, is it?" said Johnny, smiling.

He looked around at members of his racing team and added, "Everyone loves a winner, right?" His team laughed.

"I'd love to get your autograph," said Shawn.

"For sure," said Johnny. "Give me your cap."

"Great! I can't wait to add it to my collection," said Shawn. He handed Johnny his baseball cap. "I'm trying to get autographs of all the cup winners," he added.

One of Johnny's team members handed him a silver marker. Johnny signed his name in big letters on the brim of Shawn's cap.

Shawn was so excited, he couldn't stop talking. "Thanks to my uncle Roy, I've got eight other autographs already," he said. "I even have Tim Flock's autograph. My uncle bought that one for me online."

Johnny frowned. "Tim Flock?" he asked. "Is he a racer?"

Shawn laughed. "That's a good one," he said. "But Gene thinks Herb Thomas was the best of the old timers," he went on. "Can you believe that? Buck Baker was way better, don't you think?"

"Who?" asked Johnny, handing the cap back to Shawn. "Buck who?"

"Buck Baker," said Shawn.

Johnny frowned again.

Shawn added, "You know, the winner of the cup in 1956 and 1957."

"Never heard of him," said Johnny. "I don't really know about those old guys, Shawn. I live in the present. I let the bookworms worry about the past."

Shawn turned to look at Gene. Gene just shrugged his shoulders.

"Anyway," said Johnny, "did Gene take you out on the track?"

"He sure did," said Shawn, getting excited again.

"So I guess you got to ride in the granny car, huh?" asked Johnny.

"The what?" asked Shawn.

"The granny car," said Johnny. He grinned at his team again. "That car he drives around the track like an old grandma." His team laughed.

"Um, I guess," Shawn said.

"You want to see a real car go around the track?" said Johnny. "You come hang with me tomorrow. See you later. It's time to meet my fans."

Johnny strutted off toward a group of reporters.

Chapter 7

DISAPPOINTMENT

"Are you going to hang with Johnny tomorrow?" asked Gene as he and Shawn left the media tent.

Shawn didn't say anything. He kept his head down while he walked.

"Are you all right?" asked Gene.

"I'm fine," said Shawn.

"Don't let it get to you," said Gene.

"Don't let what get to me?" asked Shawn.

"The way Johnny acted back there," said Gene.

"It's no big deal," said Shawn.

They kept walking toward the garage. "It's not easy when we meet our heroes," said Gene. "They never measure up to our high expectations."

"They sure make Johnny seem different on TV," said Shawn. "I thought he was a nice guy."

"Johnny is a nice guy," said Gene.

"He didn't act nice," said Shawn. He kicked a rock across the pavement. "Why are you sticking up for him, Gene? Why are you defending him? He called your car a granny car. I wanted to punch him for saying that."

Gene shook his head.

"That wouldn't have done much good, kid," said Gene. "Johnny's just young, that's all."

"He didn't know anything about the old-time racers," said Shawn.

"He'll learn to respect the sport more as he gets older," said Gene. "That's what happens."

Shawn looked at Gene. "Can I ask you a question?" he asked.

"Sure," said Gene.

"Uncle Roy told me that your crash with Johnny last season was caused by a problem with your car and that you didn't do it on purpose," said Shawn. "Is that true?"

Gene nodded. "Yeah, it is," he said.

Shawn stopped walking. "Then why didn't you tell me that?" he asked. "And why didn't you go on TV and tell everyone else?"

"I don't like spending my time talking on TV," said Gene. "I just like to race."

"But everyone calls you Mean Gene," said Shawn. "Everyone hates you."

"Really? They hate me?" asked Gene.

"Well, I don't know," said Shawn. "Maybe they don't hate you, but they don't like you very much either."

"That's just the media hype and buzz. All I can do is be myself," said Gene. "True fans will figure out that I'm a nice guy. I won't be Mean Gene forever."

"I hope you're right," said Shawn. "But for now, can I give you some advice?"

"Shoot," said Gene.

"You should smile once in a while," said Shawn. "The fans like that."

"I'll give it some thought," said Gene.

Shawn laughed. Gene smiled, and they walked into the garage.

Chapter 8

RACE DAY

Race day was even better than Shawn imagined it would be. As Roy drove him to pit road, Shawn couldn't believe what he was seeing.

There were people everywhere. Crew members rushed wildly from their trailers to the track. People were grilling hamburgers and hot dogs next to their RVs in the middle of the speedway. And thousands of fans were in the grandstand bleachers waiting for the race to begin.

"Hey, Shawn," said Bob as Shawn and Roy pulled into the pits. "Glad you could make it."

"Thanks for letting me hang out on pit road," said Shawn.

"Gene wouldn't have it any other way," said Bob. "Now, hustle back to the dressing room and get ready."

"Get ready for what?" asked Shawn.

"You're a team member," said Bob. "You need to put this on, and get ready to go to work." Bob held up a full driver's suit. It was just like the one Gene wore.

"Awesome!" said Shawn.

"Hurry up and get ready," said Bob. "You're our junior race member. We need you."

As soon as he was dressed, Shawn settled onto a stool behind the pit wall to watch the race. Bob gave Shawn a set of headphones so he could listen to the conversations between Gene and his crew during the race.

Gene was having a great race day. Just twenty minutes into the race, he was only a few cars behind Johnny.

On lap 55, Gene's car came into the pits and recorded the fastest pit time of the day.

Gene gave a thumbs-up to Shawn as his car flew back onto the track in second place. Johnny was still in first.

Finally, on lap 150 Gene made an amazing move to the outside and took Johnny by surprise. He pushed his car past Johnny's and snagged a lead that he never gave up.

Mean Gene finished the race several seconds ahead of Johnny Pride and won the Talladega Cup. "Gene's the man!" shouted Shawn as Gene crossed the finish line. "Gene Pederson is the man!"

Gene took his car for a victory lap around the track, holding the checkered flag out his car window. Then Shawn watched as Gene crawled out his window and got sprayed and splashed with energy drinks by his crew.

After several minutes of celebrating, Gene stepped onto the podium to accept the Talladega Trophy. The race sponsors presented Gene with a huge gold cup. Gene raised it above his head as cameras flashed all around.

Chapter 9

CELEBRATING VICTORY

When the cheers had died down, one of the race officials climbed onto the podium with a microphone to interview Gene.

"So, Gene," said the official. "How does it feel to win your first cup race?"

"It feels great," said Gene. "Even better than I thought it would. But I've got to say, I've been proud of all my races this year. This just happened to be the first one I got lucky enough to win."

"When you won today, you beat fan favorite Johnny Pride," said the official. "Are you worried that his fans are going to like you even less after this race?"

"Johnny's a great guy," said Gene. "He's a top racer, and he has millions of fans. He's a good friend, and I respect him. But today I just happened to get lucky and beat him. The next race he might beat me. He makes me better, and I think I make him better."

"No more Mean Gene Pederson?" asked the official.

"If you want to keep calling me Mean Gene that's up to you," said Gene. "But my fans know who I really am." Gene looked out into the crowd. "Isn't that right, Shawn?"

The official looked confused. "Who's Shawn?" he asked.

"He's my junior racer," said Gene. "And I hope he would say he's my newest fan."

Gene looked back at the crowd. "Shawn, are you out there?" he called out.

Shawn stood up as tall as he could. The people in the crowd looked around to see who Gene was talking to. Shawn raised his hand. "I'm right here!" he yelled.

"Get up here, Shawn!" Gene said.

A path opened up as Shawn worked his way to the front of the crowd. He climbed onto the podium and stood next to Gene.

Gene shook Shawn's hand as fans cheered. Then Gene said, "Shawn, this is for you."

Gene pointed at his mouth. Then he grinned the biggest grin of his racing career.

Shawn smiled back.

Chapter 10

TOUGH COMPETITION

Back at Shawn's hometown kart track, Shawn headed into the garage. As he walked in, he saw his biggest rival, Freddy. "Hey, Freddy," Shawn called, jogging over to Freddy.

"What's up?" said Freddy, turning around.

"I want to talk to you about your driving," said Shawn.

"My driving?" asked Freddy. "I don't think I care what you have to say about my driving."

"Listen," said Shawn. "I'm sorry for being a jerk before."

Freddy looked surprised. "Why the change?" he asked.

"After spending time with Gene Pederson last week, I figured out that trash talking and bragging about winning isn't cool," said Shawn.

"Gene Pederson? Mean Gene?" asked Freddy.

"I don't call him that anymore," said Shawn.

"You said he was a loser," said Freddy.

"Yeah," said Shawn, "but I was wrong."

"So what does this have to do with me?" asked Freddy.

"It has everything to do with you," said Shawn. "Like I said, I hope that we can be friends."

"That's cool, I guess," said Freddy.

"And friends share racing tips with each other, right?" asked Shawn.

"I suppose," said Freddy.

"Well," said Shawn. "I think if you try something different on your third turn . . ."

Shawn went on to tell Freddy about all the strategies he had used in past races to beat him.

Freddy seemed grateful. He even thanked Shawn. But now, Shawn knew he might lose.

Soon he was back on the track, racing Freddy. With one lap to go, Shawn tried everything to get around Freddy. But Freddy wouldn't let up. At every turn, he stopped Shawn from passing him.

On the third turn, Freddy kept his kart under control. He banked it wide, and then shot quickly through turns three and four. Shawn didn't have a chance. He watched as Freddy crossed the finish line in front of him.

After the race, Shawn took his place on the second-place podium as Freddy stepped onto the winner's spot. Freddy accepted his trophy and smiled as several cameras snapped his picture.

"I bet you wish you hadn't given me that advice," Freddy said with a smile.

"Nope, I'm glad I did," said Shawn, laughing. "I'll get you next time. I'll just have to push myself harder. Like a good friend of mine once said, 'I make you better, and you make me better.'"

SPEED CAMP

**TEXT BY
J. GUNDERSON**

DYLAN SMITH

Car 2
Team Smith/Turner
Position: Car Designer/Driver

TABLE OF
CONTENTS

Chapter 1

READY TO RACE

"This summer is going to be great," I told my best friend, Robby, as we walked home from school. It was our last day of seventh grade and the start of our summer vacation. We always looked forward to summer, of course. But this year was special.

This year, Robby and I were going to the best summer camp ever. We'd get to spend our days around race cars at Kyle "The Killer" Kingston's Top Speed Race Camp.

At the camp, kids learn all about stock race cars. Everybody works toward the summer's big event when campers race for the camp championship. The whole thing was a dream come true, if you asked me.

But one of the best things about the camp would be meeting Kyle Kingston. He was one of my favorite NASCAR drivers, and Robby's too. This year, he retired from driving in NASCAR and opened the camp. I couldn't wait to meet him.

In spite of his nickname, The Killer seemed like one of the nicest guys on the track. He laughed more than any of the drivers I'd seen on TV.

"I wonder why he's called The Killer. He's seems so friendly," I said.

"It's ironic," Robby answered.

"Ironic?" I asked.

"Yeah, you know, when something is the opposite of what it really means." Robby paused, and I knew what was coming. "You didn't know that, Dylan?"

I rolled my eyes. Sometimes being best friends with Robby was not easy. Sure, he was smart, but he acted like he was a genius.

He rubbed it in everyone's faces, especially mine. He was smarter than me, faster than me, and all-around better than me. Or so he liked to tell me.

"I suppose you were too busy drawing your pictures to pay attention in class," Robby went on.

He pretended like he was annoyed, but I could tell he was jealous. The one thing I was better at than Robby was drawing.

I could draw anything and make it look real. My favorite thing to draw, of course, was race cars. I'd been drawing them since I was a little kid.

Drawings of all kinds of cars hung in my room: sprint cars, Formula 1 cars, and my favorite, stock cars. My dream was to become a NASCAR driver.

Robby loved cars just as much as I did, but he couldn't draw. Instead of drawings, his room was filled with photos cut from racing magazines. He said he thought his room was better. But I knew that deep down, he'd rather draw his own cars.

Robby and I lived on the same street. As we neared our mailboxes, we saw red-and-yellow striped envelopes in our boxes.

"Top Speed Race Camp!" we shouted in unison. We tore open our letters.

I read aloud. "Kyle Kingston can't wait to kick-start The Killer's Camp for Kids . . ."

"Somebody likes alliteration!" said Robby.

"Likes what?" I asked.

"Alliteration," he repeated. "You know, when words start with the same sound. You didn't know that?"

I ignored him and kept reading. "During your two weeks at camp, you will work in teams of two. Each team will design a sprint car, with help from Kyle, of course!"

I imagined Robby and me, driving in the best-looking stock car the world had ever seen.

The partner pairings were listed at the bottom of the letter. I scanned the names, looking for my own.

"Dylan Smith and . . . and Joe Turner," I read. I sighed. "I guess you and I won't be partners."

Robby folded his letter. "My partner is someone named Kevin," he said.

He looked disappointed for a minute, but then he smiled. "My team will win!" he said. "We'll leave you and Joe in the dust!"

I frowned. "How do you know? You've never even met Joe," I told him.

"I don't have to," said Robby. "I'm the best."

Chapter 2

OFF TO CAMP

By the first day of camp, I'd forgotten my disappointment about not being paired with Robby. In some ways, I was actually glad.

I'd been friends with Robby since first grade. And he usually decided what we did and how we'd do it. It would be nice to have a change.

My parents drove Robby and me to the camp. Robby talked the whole time.

He went on and on about how his team was going to win the final race. I saw my parents rolling their eyes, but they didn't say anything.

Top Speed Race Camp was even more amazing than I'd dreamed. The driveway to the camp looked like a race track. Green and red flags told us when to stop and when to go.

Traffic cones lined the drive, and we had to swerve around them. Dad had a blast, but Mom looked like she was going to lose her lunch.

The camp buildings were painted in bright colors. There were glowing greens and yellows, bright reds and blues. Flags flew everywhere. Loudspeakers hung over the yard and the buildings. But they didn't play music.

Instead, they played recordings of revving engines, honking horns, and cheering crowds. Mom covered her ears.

Outside the main office building, a man wearing a racing suit handed us our own suits and helmets. My suit was red with number 2 on it. Robby's was green, with number 16.

"There goes my hair!" Mom complained as she put on her helmet.

She was clearly not as excited as Robby and I were.

After we put on our gear, the man led us inside. Small race cars, sort of like bumper cars at a carnival, lined the wall.

We each hopped in one and zoomed around the side of the building. When I say zoomed, I really mean chugged. A baby could move faster than those cars.

Behind the building and down the hill was the race track. It was all I could do not to jump out of my little race car and run to the track. I could tell Robby felt the same way.

In the middle of the race track was the pit. That's where drivers pull over during a race to change tires. I didn't see any cars, but I saw tons of kids and parents standing around. All of them wore helmets and suits like ours.

Kyle Kingston stood in the middle of the pit, telling a story. "Back in 1976, I was racing in the Daytona 500," he began.

We listened as he told about the races he'd competed in and the points he'd earned. Then he told us about his father, who had raced in some of the first stock car races at Daytona Beach, Florida.

Finally, he was done with his stories.

"All right, kids!" shouted Kyle. "Say goodbye to your parents. Then find the kid wearing the same number and color as you. That is your partner. When you find your partner, you can take off your helmet."

I looked around for a boy in bright red. I saw him, waving excitedly at me.

"Hi," he said when I reached him.

"Hey," I said. "I'm Dylan. You must be Joe?"

He nodded and took off his helmet. Out popped two long braids.

I couldn't believe it. Staring back at me was a girl.

Chapter 3

AN UNEXPECTED PARTNER

"I can't believe my partner's a girl," I moaned as Robby and I got ready for bed.

Robby had jumped up onto the top bunk as soon as we got in our room. He never even bothered to ask if I minded sleeping on the bottom bunk.

Robby pounded his fists against the side of his bunk bed in laughter. "Kevin and I are really going to beat you now!" he gasped between laughs.

"Ten o'clock. Lights out!" called the camp counselor.

"Why didn't you know it was a girl when you saw the letter?" Robby whispered.

I shrugged in the dark. "Joe is a boy's name," I said.

"Yeah, J-O-E," Robby said. "But girls named Jo spell it J-O. You didn't know that?"

"I just didn't think there would be girls here!" I told him.

Jo wasn't even the only girl at camp. There were a lot of girls. It seemed sort of weird to me. I didn't know any girls back home who were interested in cars.

"There's no way you'll ever win the final race now," Robby said. He laughed. "You might as well just go home."

The counselor strode toward us. "Hey, motor mouth," he barked. "Keep it quiet!"

The loudspeakers around the camp still played. Instead of revving engines, the soft hum of idling engines surrounded us.

Robby fell asleep right away, but I lay awake. So far, race camp was nothing like I expected.

The next day we paired up and walked to the garage to see our cars. Jo said hi right away, but I didn't say anything. As we walked toward the garage, I shot her a few dirty looks. She was ruining my time at camp.

Jo caught me glaring at her. "If you're trying to scare me, it won't work," she said.

"I wasn't . . ." I began, but then I stopped. What did I care what she thought?

"So I was thinking," Jo went on, "I could paint the car if you want. I have some designs in mind, and I'm pretty good at drawing."

I shrugged. "Whatever," I said.

"Don't say whatever! We're a team!" she said. "I just figured that you wouldn't want to. Boys usually don't like art and drawing and stuff."

"Whatever," I said again.

"Hey, girlie, you might want to let Dylan do the painting," Robby interrupted. He and Kevin were right behind us, listening to our every word. "He's pretty great at art."

Jo looked at me. "Is that true?" she asked.

I shrugged.

Jo turned to Robby. "By the way, my name is not girlie," she told him. "It's Jo. And thanks for the information. Dylan here doesn't talk too much."

Robby snickered. "No problem," he said. "I'm just trying to help out the losing team."

Chapter 4

IN THE GARAGE

Inside the garage, Jo and I stared at our car. "It's beautiful!" Jo whispered.

"It sure is," I said.

But it really wasn't anything yet. Our car looked like everyone else's.

Stock cars are my favorite cars because they look like regular cars. But, below the surface, they aren't regular at all. They are made of fiberglass instead of metal.

Big engines and smooth tires called slicks turn stock cars into fast race cars.

Jo popped the hood and peered at the engine. "Oh. It's only a four-cylinder," she said. "Most race cars have eight cylinders. We won't be able to go very fast."

Since we were still kids, Kyle wouldn't let us race as fast as the professionals did.

"Slow racing is better than no racing," I said.

"I can't wait to drive it!" Jo exclaimed.

"Me either," I agreed. In my excitement, I'd forgotten that I didn't like Jo.

As Jo fiddled with the engine, I asked, "So why do you like cars so much?"

Jo's head popped up and she glared at me. "What do you mean?" she asked.

I didn't say anything.

"Just because I'm a girl —" she snapped.

"I didn't mean —" I started to say. But then I stopped. That really was what I'd meant.

Jo's glare faded. "Oh, it's okay," she said. "I guess I'm interested in cars for the same reasons you are. I love to go fast. And I love learning how engines work. My dream is to be like Janet Guthrie."

"Who's that?" I asked.

"What? She was the first woman to race in the Daytona 500 and the Indy 500. You didn't know that?" Jo asked.

Here we were. Robby all over again.

"No, I didn't know that!" I shouted. All my bottled-up anger at Robby exploded. I'd never shouted at Robby before. Now I was shouting at Jo.

Jo looked embarrassed. "Chill out, Dylan. I'm sorry," she said. She held up the hood and motioned to me. "Do you want to take a look?"

"Um, I really don't know that much about engines. I love cars and racing, but when it comes to engines, I don't know how they work," I admitted.

Jo shrugged. "Fine by me," she said. "I love engines. Why don't I be the head mechanic, and you be the head designer? Deal?" She held out a greasy hand.

"Deal," I said, shaking her hand.

A voice came over the door of our stall. "Hey! Look at you holding hands. How sweet!"

It was Robby.

"We were shaking hands, not holding hands," snapped Jo.

"Men shake hands. Not silly girls," Robby told her. "Why aren't you at home with your mommy, playing with your dollies?"

Behind him, Kevin chuckled.

"Stop it!" I said. Both Robby and Jo looked surprised.

"Why are you defending her? She's just a girl. She shouldn't even be here. This is a boys' camp," Robby said.

"She knows more about cars than you do," I said.

"No one knows more about cars than I do," Robby said, glaring at me. "Just you wait until the race," he continued. "You'll be eating our dust."

After he left, Jo turned to me. "Well," she said brightly, "he has a great attitude, don't you think?"

Chapter 5

THE TEST DRIVE

That night, Robby and I didn't speak to each other. At dinner, he ignored me. He sat with Kevin and the other boys. I could've sat by Jo, but then I would have had to sit at the girls' table. If Robby and I ever started speaking again, I'd never hear the end of it. Instead I went outside and ate my sandwich on the tire swing.

I thought about the first day of camp, how excited Robby and I had been. I remembered how we whispered even after the counselor called lights out. Now we weren't even speaking to each other. I was miserable.

But over the next few days, I had no time to mope. I was too busy. Every day, Jo and I worked on our car.

It was great working with Jo. For once, I got to talk about my own opinions. If Jo and I disagreed about something, we figured out a way to work it out. If Robby had been my partner, I probably would have just given in.

One thing we didn't disagree about at all was the paint job. "I was thinking we need to choose some great colors for our car," said Jo.

"For sure!" I said.

"The other kids will probably choose the usual race car colors. Bright yellows, greens, and reds," said Jo.

"Well, I've been thinking," I started. "What about metallic blue, black, and silver?"

"Perfect!" said Jo, before I could even finish describing the car's colors.

All the kids got to paint the cars themselves, with an adult watching, of course. We wore special masks so we wouldn't breathe in the paint.

We painted silver stripes along the side of the car, with stars exploding at the end of the stripes, like sparks.

"It's like something from the future," I told Jo.

After hours of work, our car was done. It was time to test our cars on the race track.

"You should be the first one to drive," Jo said.

"No, you should," I said. I really wanted to be the first to drive our car, but I knew Jo wanted to, too.

I heard Robby and Kevin arguing next to us. "I want to drive!" Robby yelled, stomping his foot.

He was used to getting his own way. If I'd been his partner, I would have let him drive first.

"Let's flip a coin," Jo suggested. She tossed a quarter into the air.

"Heads," I called.

Jo looked down. "Heads," she said.

At the track, we gathered around Kyle. "The first thing you need to know about racing is to never do anything stupid," he said. "When I was racing, way back in 1979 . . ."

Everyone moaned. All of us were excited to get on the track, and now Kyle was going off on another of his stories.

"Okay, okay," Kyle said when he realized no one was listening.

He handed out helmets to each of us. "The helmet is very important," he said. "In case of a crash, your head needs to be protected."

Next he started handing out fire suits. "Drivers need to wear fire suits," Kyle explained. "If the car catches fire, the suit protects you until you can get out."

I put on my helmet. Then I jumped through the window of the car.

"We're ready to rumble," said Kyle.

Chapter 6

FLAGGED DOWN

I turned the ignition, and the car roared to life. I loved the sound of the revving engine. It was a sound I'd heard my whole life at the races.

"Make two laps," Kyle said. "And remember, this is not a race. Stay in your own lanes. Back when I was just learning to drive —"

But his words were cut off by the waving green flag. I pushed the gas. The car rumbled down the track.

Robby was in the lane next to me. I waved at him, but he didn't even glance my way.

I didn't have time to worry about it. There I was, in the very race car Jo and I had painted. And I was driving around a track, just like a professional driver.

As we neared the first curve, I saw Robby waving at me and pointing.

"What?" I shouted, slowing down.

He laughed and sped ahead of me. Then he swerved into my lane.

"Hey!" I shouted. I had to step on my brakes so I wouldn't hit him.

"What are you doing?" I muttered.

The officials waved a red flag, which meant we were supposed to stop. Everyone stopped, except Robby. He sped around the track.

Kyle ran toward the race track, waving a black flag at him. The black flag meant that a car was in trouble or had broken the rules.

Robby finally stopped. Everyone within miles could hear Kyle yelling, "A red flag means stop!"

"I didn't see the flag," Robby argued. He didn't like being told he was wrong.

"Always pay attention to the flags," Kyle told him. "And I told you to stay in your own lane!"

The green flag waved again, and we continued our laps. When we were finished, we pulled into the pits and got out.

Robby looked around at the other kids with a champion's grin on his face. He was waiting for everyone to cheer.

"That was awesome, Robby," said Kevin. But no one else agreed.

"Why did you do that?" one of the other boys said to him.

"Yeah. What were you thinking?" asked another. "You'll get disqualified from the final race if you break the rules."

"Yes," interrupted Kyle. "And you won't be the only one disqualified. Your teammate will be, too."

"What?" said Kevin. His grin disappeared. He turned to Robby. "Don't ever do that again!" Kevin said.

But Robby just grinned smugly.

He looked at me. "See?" he said. "I told you you'd be eating my dust."

"Just wait until tomorrow's race," I said. "Then we'll see who's eating whose dust!"

Robby couldn't hide his look of surprise. I'd never stood up to him before.

I guess I was learning more at race camp than I'd bargained for.

Chapter 7

THE HEAT IS ON

I was mad at Robby, but I missed talking to him. It might be hard to see why, but he wasn't always putting me down. We usually had a great time hanging out together. And he was the only one who truly understood my love of racing.

After lights out that night, I leaned up toward Robby's bunk. "Good luck at the race tomorrow," I said.

He didn't answer. But later, as I was drifting off to sleep, I heard him say, "You, too."

The next day, the camp was flooded with people. Parents, grandparents, brothers, and sisters filled the grandstand. Everyone was there to see the big race.

Campers were divided into heats to race. The top three from each heat would advance to the final race. The final race was a relay. One teammate drove the first ten laps, and the second teammate drove the last ten.

Our race was going to be different than professional stock car races. In professional races, one driver drives the whole race. And they drive a lot more than just 20 laps. At the Daytona 500, one of the biggest stock car races in America, the driver drives 200 laps.

Jo and I flipped a coin to see who would drive in the first heat. "Tails," Jo called.

The coin landed tails-up. Jo looked nervous as she snapped on her helmet. "Here I go," she said.

I saw Kevin putting on his helmet. Robby hadn't won his coin toss either.

At the flag, the cars sped off. I'd wanted to drive in the heat, but I cheered Jo on.

Watching our car speed around the track was almost as exciting as being the driver. The sun gleamed on the blue hood. The silver sparks we'd painted truly sparkled.

I watched as Jo rounded the first curve. She was ahead of the pack. But as she came out of the curve, she lost speed.

Car 20 was gaining on her. Then 20 passed her, and so did Kevin in car number 16. My heart lunged to my throat. If Jo didn't win the first heat, I wouldn't get to drive at all.

"A girl at the wheel is never a good thing," Robby said next to me.

I ignored him. "Come on, Jo!" I yelled.

"You've got the best-looking car out there, though," Robby added.

I was surprised. Why was he admitting that our car looked the best?

Then I figured it out. "You want to kiss up to me so I let you win tomorrow," I accused. "Is that your plan?"

Robby looked hurt. "No, I just —"

I interrupted him. "Well, you can just forget about it!" I shouted and turned back to the race.

Jo was creeping ahead. It was the last lap and her last chance.

Jo and Kevin were neck and neck, barreling toward the checkered finish line. Then, just before the finish, car number 20 came from behind and plunged forward.

The crowd screamed as the three cars blasted through the finish.

"Folks, I've never seen anything like it," Kyle said into the microphone. "It's a three-way tie. Cars number 2, number 16, and number 20 will advance to the finals."

Jo jumped out of the car and ran toward me. "I did it, Dylan!" she yelled, jumping up and down. "We're in!"

Chapter 8

TRACK TROUBLE

The heats were over, and the final relay race was about to begin. The crowd roared in excitement. The cars were already in place, staggered around the track. The ones with the fastest times were placed toward the front.

Kyle stepped up to the microphone. He said, "Welcome, one and all, to The Killer's Grand Tournament! And now, the racers."

The crowd roared even louder.

Kyle continued. "Behind the wheel of car number 16, Kevin and Robby! Driving car number 2, Jo and Dylan!"

Jo and I stood by our car, waving at the crowd.

"Good luck," I called as she hopped through the window. She gave me a thumbs-up.

A horn blew, and the green flag flew. Everyone cheered, and the cars took off.

Jo shot ahead, taking the turns easily. On the straights she rocketed far ahead of the other drivers, even Kevin. My throat was hoarse from cheering.

But then it happened. On her final lap, as she neared the curve, the car lurched toward the side of the track. "No!" I cried.

Jo didn't crash. She managed to get the car back on track. But not before Kevin soared past her. "Yes!" I heard Robby shout.

Jo rumbled toward the pit, so we could switch spots. I buckled my helmet and got ready. The pit crew rushed to the car to change the tires. The slick racing tires wore out easily, so they had to be changed during the race.

Jo jumped out of the car, and I jumped in.

"I think the tire alignment is a little off," she said. "But there's no time to fix it. Just hold tight to the steering wheel."

I slid into the car and fastened my belt. I saw Robby speeding out of the pit.

"Ready!" called one of the mechanics.

I punched the gas. The race was on.

Robby was right ahead of me. I followed him closely, drafting to help gain speed.

The straightaways were fun. I loved feeling the speed of the car under me.

But I got nervous during the curves. Curves were the most dangerous part of any auto race. I'd seen many drivers take a curve too fast, lose control, and crash.

And since my tire alignment was off, it was trickier than usual.

I held the wheel tightly as I rounded the curve. I was still on Robby's heels.

When we reached the straight, I sped up and pulled next to Robby. I didn't dare look at him. I concentrated on my speed. Then I glanced over. He had fallen behind.

But ahead of us was another curve. As I neared it, I felt the car shift slightly under me. The wheels wanted to turn toward the outside of the oval track.

I clutched the wheel and tried to hold steady, but it was too late.

Chapter 9

FINAL LAP

I slammed on the brakes as I hit the fence. I put the car in reverse, but I was stuck. The car wouldn't move. In my rearview mirror I saw Robby. I expected him to fly past me, but he didn't. He was heading straight for me.

"What are you doing?" I yelled, even though I knew he couldn't hear me. I signaled for him to go around me. But he pulled up right behind me and stopped.

Then he bumped against my rear fender.

At first I thought he was trying to wreck my car. Then I realized what he was doing. He was helping me get back in the race.

I twisted the wheel to the left. He bumped against me again, and I gave the car gas. Finally, the front wheels took hold of the pavement. I gunned the gas again. My car whirred into motion. I still had a chance.

Cars had passed us while we were stopped, but there were still three laps to go. There was enough time to catch up. I could still win. But so could Robby.

I gained speed on the straightaway. I weaved around car number 12, then car number 20. Robby did the same. The white flag waved, signaling the final lap. Robby and I were neck-and-neck. I clutched the wheel as I turned the final curve.

Robby and I were both focused on one goal: the finish line. The crowd cheered as we sped over the checkered finish line. The flags waved.

"Number 2 is number one! Number 2 wins!" Kyle yelled.

I had won! I pulled into the pits, with Robby right behind me.

Jo was jumping up and down, screeching with happiness. "We won! We won!" she screamed.

Then I saw Robby. He took off his helmet and rubbed his head, scowling. "Second place," he said to Kevin. "We lost."

I walked over to him. "Thanks," I said.

He smiled, but I could tell he was not happy. "Congratulations," he said.

"I couldn't have done it without your help," I told him. Robby shrugged.

Kyle jogged up to us. He clapped Robby on the back. "Nice work out there," he said. "You showed great sportsmanship by helping Dylan."

Robby shrugged again. "Well, he's my best friend," he said.

"That's right!" I agreed, and finally Robby smiled a real smile.

As we walked toward the grandstand to meet our parents, Robby turned to me. "I'm sorry about how I've been acting," he said. "I guess I was just jealous."

"Jealous?" I repeated.

Robby looked away. "Yeah. I wish I'd been paired with Jo," he admitted. "She's so . . . so cool!"

"I sure am!" Jo said from behind us.

"I'm glad we're friends again," I told Robby.

I looked behind us at the pits, where our race cars were lined up.

Then I thought of something. "I love the words 'race car,'" I said. "Together, they're a palindrome, you know."

"A what?" asked Robby.

"A palindrome," I repeated. "You know, when something is spelled the same backward and forward. R-A-C-E-C-A-R."

Robby looked thoughtful. "Oh," he nodded.

"You didn't know that?" I said.

Robby and Jo looked at me, and the three of us burst out laughing.

STOCK CAR SABOTAGE

TEXT BY ERIC STEVENS

DANNY MASON

Car 9
Team "Clean" Cole Mason
Position: Garage Custodian

TABLE OF CONTENTS

Chapter 1

"CLEAN" COLE MASON

In garage 9 at the River City Raceway, Danny Mason pushed a broom across the floor. He wasn't doing much good sweeping, though. His attention was on the TV monitors that lined the walls. "Come on, Cole!" he shouted at the TVs.

Danny's older brother, "Clean" Cole Mason, was driving car 9. Today's race was the River City Classic. Cole had to do well if he hoped to win the series of races.

Now he was in third place. It was good enough to stay high in overall league standings. But Danny still hoped his brother would come in first.

Before long, the checkered flag was waving as Harvey Nickel in car 14 drove across the finish line.

Close behind him was Scott Stanley in car 11. Clean Cole Mason came in third.

"Darn!" Danny said to himself. Still, Cole had done well. He was one of the best racers on the regional circuit. If he kept racing the way he had for the last few months, he'd make it to NASCAR.

Danny dropped the broom. He jogged out of the garage to wave at his brother as car 9 pulled in. The car came to a stop in the garage.

Some of the pit crew helped Cole climb out. "Great race, Cole!" Danny called out. He gave his brother a high five.

"Thanks, bro," Cole said. He pulled off his helmet. He was smiling, but Danny could tell his brother wasn't feeling very happy.

"Are you disappointed about coming in third?" Danny asked.

Cole shook his head slowly. "Harvey Nickel," he said. "He's just too good."

"You haven't been able to beat him this series, have you?" Danny asked.

"No," Cole answered. "I mean, Scott Stanley is no big deal. I think we're well matched. I outrace him sometimes, and he outraces me sometimes. But Harvey . . . I just can't seem to pass him."

"Do you think he has a better machine?" Danny asked. He had noticed that a lot of the guys in the pit crews said "machine" when they talked about cars. Danny wanted to sound like all of the other guys.

"I think our machines are even," Cole replied.

"Maybe you should let me on the pit crew!" Danny said. "I'll cut your pit time in half."

Cole laughed. "You know you're too young to be in the pit crew, Danny," he said. "You're only fourteen. Wait a couple of years."

Danny shrugged. "It was worth a shot," he said. "So why does Harvey keep winning?"

Cole put a gloved hand on his little brother's shoulder. "Some drivers," he said, "are just better than others. But, boy, I'd do just about anything to beat him once."

Chapter 2

THE EIGHTH MAN

The following weekend, race time came around again. This time, the Mason boys were at the Lakeville Speedway.

"You ready to race, Cole?" Danny asked.

Cole pulled on his helmet as the pit crew pushed car 9 out of the garage.

"Sure am, Danny," Cole replied. "I have a really good feeling about the race today. I just know I'm going to beat Harvey Nickel this time."

Danny patted his brother on the back and headed into the garage to watch the race on the TV monitors.

About halfway through the race, Danny stood in the garage. He was leaning on his push broom, staring at the monitors. He watched car 9, Clean Cole's car. Cole was driving hard, but just like last week, he couldn't pass Harvey Nickel.

Suddenly, Danny felt a hand on his shoulder. He turned. It was Jim Yolk, one of the new guys on Cole's pit crew. Danny knew that Jim was the eighth man on the crew.

Normally, only seven men were allowed over the wall and onto the track during a pit stop. Sometimes, though, an eighth man could go over.

The eighth man wasn't allowed to do everything. He could only do things like bring water for the driver or clean the windshield. Most of the time, though, Jim didn't have anything to do during a pit stop.

Jim was a tall, broad man, and he smiled all the time. It wasn't a nice smile, though. It was creepy. Danny thought there was something weird about him.

"Hi, Danny," Jim said.

"Hi," Danny replied.

"Your brother is really giving his all out there today," Jim went on, glancing at the TV monitors.

"I guess so," Danny said. "He already has Scott Stanley beat. I know he wants to beat Harvey Nickel, too."

Jim winked. "He sure does," he said. "I'd say he'd do just about anything to beat Harvey Nickel, wouldn't you?"

Danny shrugged. "I don't know," he said. He thought about it for a moment. "Well, I don't think he'd do anything."

Jim patted Danny's shoulder and turned to leave. "Well, don't worry too much," Jim said. "I have a feeling he's going to win this race."

With that, Jim Yolk headed back to his place with the pit crew.

Danny watched the rest of the race closely.

With three laps to go, Harvey was still in first place, and Cole was still in second. They led the pack by a long way, but Cole was no closer to getting around Harvey.

"I guess Jim was wrong," Danny mumbled to himself.

But suddenly, as Harvey came around a curve, his engine cut out completely. Car 14 just rolled to a stop!

Danny gasped as Cole sped toward the stopped car. His brother was a great driver. He was able to steer around the stopped car and take the lead.

But the third-place driver, Lou Dyver in car 5, couldn't swerve in time. He rear-ended Harvey's car, sending both cars into the wall!

Chapter 3

AN ACCIDENT?

After the crash, the warning flag came down right away, and the other drivers slowed to a stop. Moments later, Harvey and Lou climbed out of their cars and waved to the crowd. They were both okay, but out of the race.

Danny sighed with relief. "At least no one was hurt," he said to himself.

Soon the race started again, with only two laps to go. Cole won easily.

Car 9 pulled into the garage. Danny watched as the crowd went crazy.

"How about that, Danny?" Cole said after he climbed out of the car. "Lucky break, huh?"

Danny scratched his chin. "For you, sure," he said. "Not so lucky for Harvey, though."

Cole laughed. "That's true," he said. "He's not hurt, though, so it's okay." Cole mussed Danny's hair and walked off to change.

Danny frowned. He wasn't so sure it was okay.

He strolled down the infield until he saw Eddie Paulsen. Eddie worked on Lou Dyver's pit crew. He was the Dyver crew's jack man, the toughest job on the crew.

It was Eddie's job to get the car up off the ground quickly during a pit stop so the tire changers could do their work. It wasn't an easy job. The scariest part was when the car pulled in. The jack man had to run to the side of the car as the driver pulled in — heading right at him!

Danny didn't think he would ever have the nerve to run across the path of a speeding car. He would be too nervous that the driver wouldn't stop in time, and he would be run over.

"Hi, Eddie," Danny said. "Some race!"

"Some ending, you mean!" Eddie replied. "Lou hasn't been in the top three in about ten races. He's angry he lost his third-place finish at the last second."

"I don't blame him," Danny replied.

Danny glanced around to make sure no one else was listening. Then he leaned closer to Eddie. "Did the accident seem sort of weird to you?" Danny asked.

"What do you mean?" Eddie asked.

"Well, I was talking to Jim Yolk during the race," Danny explained. "You know Jim. The new guy on my brother's pit crew."

Eddie nodded. "Sure," he said. "I've known Jim Yolk for years. Not very well, though."

"Anyway, Jim said he was sure Cole would beat Harvey in the race," Danny went on. "Even though Cole had been behind the whole race. Plus, he's never beaten Harvey. Ever!"

"Well, he is on Cole's pit crew," Eddie said with a shrug. "Of course he wants your brother to win."

"But he was so sure Cole would win," Danny said. "It was like he knew he would win somehow. Like he knew the accident would happen."

Eddie leaned back and waved his arms. "Whoa, whoa," he said. "Are you saying Jim Yolk had something to do with Harvey's machine stalling?"

Danny scratched his chin. "Don't you think it's possible?" he asked.

Eddie smiled. "I guess it might be possible," he said. "But sometimes machines have problems. You can't just start pointing fingers."

"I guess you're right," Danny said.

"Besides," Eddie added quickly, "your brother didn't earn the nickname 'Clean' Cole by hiring shady guys to work in his pit crew. If Cole likes Jim Yolk, he must be a good guy."

Danny had to agree with that. His brother was the nicest, fairest guy on the circuit. There was no way he'd hire anyone who would make an opponent crash. Was there?

Chapter 4

LUCKY BREAK?

The next afternoon, Cole and Danny were hanging out in their garage at home. Cole tinkered with an old sports car he had been restoring, while Danny helped as much as he could.

"I can't wait to get this machine running," Cole said, looking under the hood of the car.

The car had been built in the 1960s. It was small and sleek and silver.

Cole had gotten it for a steal when he was only sixteen. But he'd been working on it for three years, and the motor still didn't turn over.

"It's going to be awesome," Danny agreed. He couldn't wait to get his own driver's license.

"So, Cole," Danny said. Cole continued to work under the hood of his car. "That was some lucky break you got yesterday, huh?"

"Huh?" Cole said. "Lucky break? What do you mean?"

"In the race," Danny added. "When Harvey stalled, and then Lou Dyver hit him."

Cole chuckled. "Oh, that," he said. "Yeah, I guess it was lucky."

"Does Harvey's crew know what happened?" Danny said. "Or do the race officials know what caused the stall?"

Cole shrugged and walked over to his tool box. "Who knows?" he said. "Listen, Danny. In this game, sometimes things go wrong. People crash. Machines stall."

Cole picked up a rag and wiped some grease from his hands.

"I guess so," Danny agreed.

"Besides," Cole went on, "I was going to pass Harvey, stall or not. I knew I was going to win that race."

"You did?" Danny asked. "How did you know?"

"I could just feel it, that's all," Cole replied. "Now let's get some lunch, okay?"

Danny followed his brother to the house. "Sure, Cole," he said. But as he walked into the house, he thought, *How did Cole know he would win? He hasn't beaten Harvey all year.*

Chapter 5

CRYING JIM YOLK

The next race was held at Willow Junction Speedway. As the teams and drivers were getting ready, Jim walked over to Danny.

"Told you Cole would win last week, didn't I?" Jim asked Danny.

Danny looked Jim right in the eyes. "Yes, you did," he replied. "You were very certain."

Jim laughed. "I sure was," he said. "You might say I knew that Harvey wouldn't be able to finish."

"Did you know Harvey Nickel was going to stall and get into a crash?" Danny asked.

Jim smirked. "Now, how would I have known something like that?" he asked. "I mean, I can't predict the future or something, can I?"

Danny was about to agree. But then Jim winked.

Then, with another sly smile, Jim turned and walked away.

* * *

"Eddie!" Danny cried out. He ran through the infield toward Lou Dyver's garage. "Eddie, where are you?"

"Whoa, there, Danny," Eddie said as he stepped out of the Dyver garage. "What's all the hollering about?"

"Eddie," Danny said as he caught his breath. "It's Jim Yolk."

Eddie rolled his eyes. "Danny, have you ever heard of the boy who cried wolf?" he asked.

"I'm not crying wolf," Danny replied. "I'm crying Jim Yolk."

"Okay, so what happened now?" Eddie asked. He crossed his arms.

"Jim just strolled right up to me and admitted he knew for sure that Cole would win last week," Danny explained.

"Didn't we go over this last weekend?" Eddie said.

"There's more," Danny said. "When I asked if Jim knew that Harvey would stall, Jim said, 'How would I have known that?' Then he winked!"

Eddie burst out laughing. "Winked?" he said through his laughter. "That's your big evidence? A wink?"

"Don't you see?" Danny protested. "The wink meant he did know, but it's a secret."

Eddie glanced at his watch. "Look, Danny," he said. "The race is going to start soon. You better get back to your brother's garage."

"You don't believe me," Danny said.

Eddie patted Danny's shoulder.

"You shouldn't watch those detective shows on TV," he said. "They're messing with your mind." Then he turned and walked off.

Danny was disappointed. He was certain Jim had something to do with the crash, but even Eddie didn't believe him. Feeling low, Danny headed back toward the Mason garage.

As he was leaving, he heard Lou Dyver talking to Harvey Nickel. Harvey wasn't in his racing gear.

"So you're not racing today, Harv?" Lou asked.

Harvey shook his head. "Nope," he replied. "The team doctor wants me to sit this week out because of the accident. It's nothing serious, but he says I should take a week off."

"That's too bad," Lou said. "Any word on what caused that stall? Really left us both in the dust, huh?"

"Sure did," Harvey replied. "It looks like there was some water in the fuel line."

"That'll do it," Lou said. "How'd you get water in your fuel?"

Harvey shrugged. "You got me," he said. "But for that amount of water to get into my fuel, something funny must have gone on."

Danny had heard enough. Now he was certain someone had messed with Harvey's car to make it stall.

And I bet a million dollars it was Jim Yolk, he thought.

Chapter 6

IN THE BAG

When Danny got back to the Mason garage, Cole was just putting his helmet on.

"Do you think you have a good shot at winning this race, Cole?" Danny asked.

"I sure do," Cole replied. Together, the brothers walked over to car 9 so Cole could climb in. "With Harvey taking the week off," Cole went on, "I'm feeling pretty certain I'll win this race."

"What about Scott Stanley?" Danny asked.

"I've beaten him lots of times," Cole replied. "I'm feeling good."

"And what about Lou Dyver?" Danny added.

"Lou Dyver?" Cole said back. "He's never even come in the top three. He's no threat."

"Last week he was in the top three," Danny pointed out, "until the crash."

"I guess that's how it goes," Cole said. "I'll tell you what. I'll watch out for Lou, if you stop worrying about everything. I've got this race in the bag."

Cole climbed into the car, and his crew rolled it out of the garage. The race was about to start.

Danny watched the cars line up for the start of the race. The engines revved, and the crowd went wild.

Jim Yolk brushed past Danny on his way to the pit.

"Hey, Jim," Danny said. He grabbed the man by the arm.

"Oh, hi, Danny," Jim replied with a smile. It gave Danny the chills. "What's up?"

"So do you think Cole will win the race today?" Danny asked.

Jim's smile got even bigger. "Let's just say I have a very, very good feeling about it," he said.

Then he reached into the pocket of his jumpsuit and pulled something out.

He held it in front of Danny for a moment, then tossed it into the air and caught it. It was a shiny metal thing, with three holes. Danny stared at the object for a moment. It looked like a short, two-headed pipe.

"Well, I better get to the pit," Jim said. He shoved the object back into his pocket. Then, with a wink at Danny, he turned and walked off.

Chapter 7

NOT SO CLEAN?

Scott Stanley and Cole drove hard the whole race. Stanley really wanted to win, but so did Cole.

Danny watched the monitors the whole race. With only a few laps to go, Cole and Stanley both went into the pits.

The Cole Mason pit crew leaped into action. They gave car 9 more fuel and four new tires. Danny watched closely. He didn't see Jim Yolk go near the car at all.

In about fifteen seconds, car 9 was already finished in the pit. The seven crewmen pushed the car out as far as they were allowed.

Cole's car and Scott Stanley's car were neck and neck as they rejoined the main track.

Suddenly, though, in the last lap, Scott Stanley's engine cut off. Stanley was able to ease his car into the infield. Meanwhile, Cole sped on to the finish line and the checkered flag.

Back in the garage, Danny watched the monitors. He could hardly believe his eyes! Another car had stalled, and once again, it had given his brother first place.

Something weird was definitely going on. Someone had to believe him now. Danny decided to find Eddie. He hadn't believed Danny before, but now he would.

As Danny ran out of the garage, car 9 pulled in. His brother Cole was at the wheel, cheering. "Another win," Danny said, but he wasn't smiling.

"Darn right," Cole replied. He climbed out of the car. "I have a shot at winning this series now, you know that?"

"Why did Stanley's car stall?" Danny asked.

"Who knows?" Cole replied. "This was a big race. His crew probably choked."

"Maybe," Danny said.

"All I know is I'm having a great run of luck," Cole added.

Someone called to Cole. He patted his brother on the back and strode off.

"Yeah, luck," Danny mumbled to himself. "If you can call it that."

* * *

"Eddie!" Danny said as he jogged up to the Dyver garage.

"I had a feeling I'd see you pretty soon," Eddie said quietly. "I'm ready to listen to you now."

"Good," Danny said.

Then he told Eddie about his meeting with Jim before the race. He described the funny metal thing Jim had put in his pocket.

Eddie nodded slowly. "Sounds like a hose splitter," he said. "That makes sense."

"Should we tell an official?" Danny asked. "Or call the police? Or something?"

"Slow down," Eddie said. "There's a right way and a wrong way to deal with this."

Eddie sat down on the metal bench in his team's garage. "I just can't believe your brother would let this happen," he said with a sigh. "I mean, he's Clean Cole Mason. He's the most honest guy in the league."

Danny scratched his chin. "Well," he said, "maybe he didn't let it happen. Jim's the newest guy on the crew. No one knows him that well."

"You think maybe he did this without your brother knowing?" Eddie asked.

Danny stared at his brother's garage. "I sure hope so," he said.

Chapter 8

CHEATING FOR SURE

Back at the Mason garage, Danny found Cole changing out of his racing jumpsuit.

"Hey, Danny," Cole said. "Where have you been?"

"I was just talking to Eddie, over at Lou Dyver's garage," Danny replied. He sat down on the bench along the wall.

"I always liked Eddie Paulsen," Cole said. "One of the best jack men in the sport. Nice guy, too."

"He called you the most honest guy in the league," Danny said.

"Did he?" Cole said. He turned to his little brother and looked him square in the eye. "That's nice. What were you two talking about, anyway?"

Danny took a deep breath. Was he really about to ask his brother if he was a cheater?

"I don't know how to say this," Danny said. "We think Jim sabotaged Scott's car today and Harvey's car last week."

Cole was stunned. "You think Jim is cheating?" he asked. "I can't believe one of my crewmen would ever do anything like that."

"That's what I thought, and Eddie, too," Danny replied. "But now I'm sure of it."

"How can you be so sure?" Cole asked.

"Jim pretty much told me," Danny said. "He even showed me a hose splitter he keeps in his pocket."

As the information sank in, Cole's face dropped. "To feed water into their fuel lines," he said quietly. "Of course. That's what happened."

"Then . . . ," Danny stammered, "you didn't know anything about this, did you?"

Cole stared at his little brother. "Danny, you didn't think I'd put Jim up to this, did you?" he asked.

Danny shrugged. "I knew you couldn't have had anything to do with it," he said. "I just didn't know how a shady guy like Jim could have been added to the team without you knowing it."

Cole sighed. Then he looked at his brother. "We have to catch Jim in the act," Cole said. "We need proof."

"If you don't mind waiting until next week's race," Danny said, "I think I have a plan."

Chapter 9

THE PLAN

The next weekend, all the teams were at the South Downs Super Speedway. This race was one of the longest of the series. Most drivers thought it was the most important race of the year.

"Harvey's back on the track today," Cole said. He and Danny were hanging out in the Mason garage before the race. "He and Scott Stanley will be my big competition."

"And Lou Dyver," Danny put in.

Cole laughed. "And Lou Dyver," he agreed.

"I wonder who Jim Yolk will hit this week, then," Danny said. "Harvey Nickel, probably."

Cole shook his head and stood up. "Hopefully no one, if your plan works, right?"

Danny smiled. "Right," he said. "Now you better get ready and get going. Jim might show up any time."

"I hope this works, Danny," Cole said. "When Jim gets caught, I want Team Mason to be the ones to catch him."

Cole pulled on his helmet. The pit crew — except for Jim — came in and pushed car 9 out of the garage. Cole followed.

Danny was alone in the garage, with the monitors, tools, and benches. And a new closed-circuit TV camera.

He was nervous. He knew Cole was really counting on him. The whole team was counting on him. In some ways, even the whole league was counting on him. If Jim's cheating wasn't stopped soon, the whole sport could be tainted.

Danny watched the TV monitors lining the garage walls. He saw Harvey Nickel's car pull up to the start line. Lou Dyver and Scott Stanley were close behind, along with his brother's car. There was still no sign of Jim Yolk when the race started.

Right away, Harvey Nickel sped off into the lead. Cole stayed right on him. During the next fifty laps, the two excellent drivers swapped first and second place over and over.

Lou Dyver and Scott Stanley fought it out for third place. Both drivers struggled to stay in the top three, but the leaders were well ahead.

"I guess Harvey is the man to beat today," a voice suddenly said.

Danny spun around. It was Jim Yolk. "Oh, hi, Jim," Danny said with a little stutter. "I didn't hear you come in."

Jim stood next to Danny and looked at the monitors. "Some race, huh?" Jim said. "A real close one. The top four drivers are really giving it their all."

"Who do you think will come out on top?" Danny asked.

Jim chuckled. "It's not who I think will win that matters," he said. "It's who I know will win. Know what I mean?"

Danny scratched his chin. "No," he said. "What do you mean?"

Jim smiled slyly. "Oh, come on, Danny boy," he said. "You know what I mean."

Jim reached into his pocket and pulled out the hose splitter. He held it up for Danny to get a good look at. "You know what this is?" Jim asked.

Danny shrugged. "A hose splitter, isn't it?" he asked.

Jim nodded. "That's right," he said. "This is what's going to make sure your older brother and Team Mason are number one this year."

Danny glanced at the camera mounted in the corner. He hoped Jim wouldn't notice it, not until he confessed completely.

"That little thing?" Danny said. "I must be stupid or something, then. Because I'm watching the race, and Harvey Nickel is still in first."

Jim glanced at the monitor. "He is now," he said. "But in a few more laps he'll enter pit lane. And when he does, I'll do my stuff."

That's not enough proof, Danny thought. Jim had said a lot already, but Danny wanted more on camera to be certain.

"What stuff do you mean?" Danny asked. He tried to sound calm and relaxed. He kept his eyes on the race, like he wasn't even interested in what Jim was saying.

"Can you keep a secret?" Jim asked with a grin. "This hose splitter lets me add a little something to any fuel line in the infield."

Danny finally looked away from the TVs and right at Jim Yolk. "What do you add?" he asked.

"Just a little water," Jim said. He was practically whispering. Danny wasn't sure the camera's small microphone would be able to pick up Jim's voice.

"To stall the engine," Danny finished. "Right? That's what would happen?"

Jim leaned back and grinned. Then he nodded. "Now you got it," he said. "Why, if it wasn't for me and my hose splitter, your brother might not even be in the top three right now."

Danny and Jim turned back to the monitors. Harvey Nickel was about to pull into the pit lane.

"Whoops, that's my cue," Jim said.

He slipped the hose splitter back into his packet. "I better get over to Nickel's fuel line and cinch this race for Clean Cole Mason."

Jim laughed as he turned to leave the garage. But he stopped laughing pretty quickly. Standing in the doorway of the garage were two security guards and a race official.

"Not so fast, Yolk," the official said. "You're busted."

Chapter 10

BUSTED

"We've been watching this whole conversation on video," the race official said. "Cole Mason himself tipped us off to your cheating, so we know you worked alone."

"Cole told you what I was doing?" Jim asked, stunned. "How did he even know?"

"Danny here figured it out," the official replied. "And he just got you to confess on camera."

The official motioned toward the men at his side. "Get him out of here!" he ordered.

The two security guards moved forward and took Jim Yolk by the arms. They escorted him out of the garage.

"Good going, Danny," the official said. "Your brother will be proud of you. You've really saved the name of Clean Cole."

* * *

Clean Cole Mason did finish first in that race, but not because Harvey Nickel couldn't compete. Nickel, Lou Dyver, and Scott Stanley all drove well. But Cole beat them all.

After the race, Cole pulled car 9 into the Mason garage. Danny was waiting there, cheering.

"You're the one who deserves the cheers, kid," Cole said. He climbed out of the car. "If it wasn't for you, Team Mason could have been run out of the sport. And now I'm pretty sure I will make it to NASCAR soon."

"I'm just sorry I ever suspected that you were involved with Jim's dirty work," Danny said.

"Don't worry about it," Cole replied. He threw an arm around his little brother's shoulders and added, "I should have kept a better eye on my crew."

Danny pointed at the camera in the corner. "Between me and the eye in the sky there," he said with a laugh, "I'd say we've got it covered."